DARK MAN

FEAR IN THE DARK

BY
PETER LANCETT

ILLUSTRATED BY JAN PEDROIETTA

Librarian Reviewer
Laurie K. Holland
Media Specialist (National Board Certified), Edina, MN
MA in Elementary Education, Minnesota State University, Mankato

Reading Consultant
Elizabeth Stedem
Educator/Consultant, Colorado Springs, CO
MA in Elementary Education, University of Denver, CO

STONE ARCH BOOKS
Minneapolis   San Diego

First published in the United States in 2008
by Stone Arch Books, A Capstone Imprint
151 Good Counsel Drive, P.O. Box 669
Mankato, Minnesota 56002
www.capstonepub.com

Library of Congress Cataloging-in-Publication Data
Lancett, Peter.
    Fear in the Dark / by Peter Lancett; illustrated by
Jan Pedroietta.
    p. cm. — (Zone Books. Dark Man)
    Summary: Dark Man needs to find the Rod of Iron, which can
control the future, before the evil Shadow Masters discover it.
    ISBN-13: 978-1-59889-869-9 (library binding)
    ISBN-10: 1-59889-869-8 (library binding)
    ISBN-13: 978-1-59889-929-0 (paperback)
    ISBN-10: 1-59889-929-5 (paperback)
    [1. Good and evil—Fiction.] I. Pedroietta, Jan, ill. II. Title.
PZ7.L2313Fe 2008
[Fic]—dc22   2007003967

Art Director: Heather Kindseth
Graphic Designer: Kay Fraser

Photo Credits
Rubberball Visuality, cover, 7, 27, 29

Printed in the United States of America in Stevens Point, Wisconsin.
032010
005744R

TABLE OF CONTENTS

In the dark and distant future, the Shadow Masters control the night. These evil powers threaten to cover the earth in complete darkness. One man has the power to stop them. He is the Dark Man — the world's only light of hope.

《 CHAPTER ONE 》

THE ROD OF IRON

The Old Man comes to see the **Dark Man.**

"They saw a **Shadow Master** in the city," the Old Man says.

6

"What does he **seek**?" the Dark Man asks.

"The **Rod of Iron**," the Old Man says.

"The Rod of Iron can **control the future**," the Dark Man says.

"So you **must** find it first," the Old Man says, as he turns to go.

CHAPTER TWO

THE GIRL

Now the Dark Man sits in a
coffee shop.

The Old Man said that a **girl**
would help him.

How will he **find** this girl?

A girl **sits** at his table.

The Dark Man **looks up** from his coffee.

He did not see her come into the coffee shop.

She looks like an **angel**.

12

"I was looking for you," the girl says.

"So now you have found me," the Dark Man says.

The **girl** stands up.

"Should we go?" she asks. "We do not have **much time**."

CHAPTER THREE

FACES IN THE SHADOWS

The girl takes the Dark Man to a
bad part of the city.

The streets are full of **broken
glass** and **trash**.

It is almost **dark**.

As they walk, the girl stays back.

"What is it?" the Dark Man asks.

"I see faces in the **shadows**," says the girl.

The Dark Man looks but **cannot see them**.

"The Shadow Master has sent things **to stop** us," the girl says.

❰ CHAPTER FOUR ❱

HORRORS IN THE DARK

The Dark Man and the girl step into a **hallway.**

There is no **light.**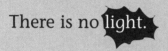

"The Rod of Iron is at the end of this hallway," the girl says.

They hear soft voices behind them.

The girl **stops.**

"I am **afraid**," she says. "It is too **dark**."

She begins to **cry**.

"Get the Rod of Iron," the Dark Man says. "I will stay here and **protect** you."

The **girl** moves forward.

The **Dark Man** can no longer see her.

He feels a push but does not move.

He **fights things** he cannot see. He does not let them pass.

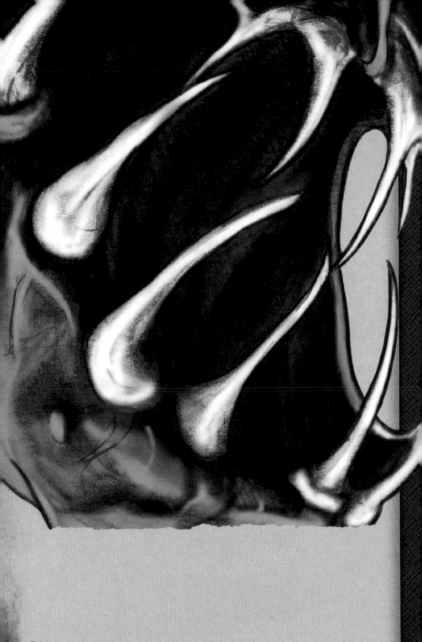

There is a **scream** that fills the hallway.

Then it is **silent**.

He calls to the girl but gets no reply. He **cannot find her**.

The Dark Man steps out into the **street**.

Does the girl have the **Rod of Iron?**

He can only **hope** that she does.

The end . . . for now.

MORE LIGHT ON IRON

Iron (EYE-urn) is one of the most common metals on Earth and in the entire universe!

At the center of Earth is a giant ball of solid iron. This iron core is about the size of the Moon!

The first iron used by humans came from meteorites, also known as space rocks.

The quality of iron found in a meteorite is rarely found on Earth. Ancient Egyptians praised the valuable rocks, calling them "iron from heaven."

In 1984, explorer Robert Peary found three giant meteorites in Greenland. Long before, native people used the iron from these space rocks for tools, knives, and harpoons.

Some people believe iron has mysterious powers. In many folk tales, the metal can chase off or keep away witches, ghosts, or evil fairies.

Others believe that iron brings good luck. Even today, people hang iron horseshoes on their walls for luck and good fortune.

If iron is lucky, then you should eat more chicken! Iron is found in the protein of all meats and helps keep your body healthy.

ABOUT THE AUTHOR

Peter Lancett was born in the city of Stoke-on-Trent, England. At age 20, he moved to London. While there, he worked for a film studio and became a partner in a company producing music videos. He later moved to Auckland, New Zealand, where he wrote his first novel, *The Iron Maiden*. Today, Lancett is back in England and continues to write his ghoulish stories.

ABOUT THE ILLUSTRATOR

Jan Pedroietta lives and works in Germany. As a boy, Pedroietta always enjoyed drawing and creating things. He also spent many hours reading his brother's comic books about cowboys and American Indians. Today, comic books still inspire Pedroietta as he continues improving his own skills.

GLOSSARY

harpoon (har-POON)—a long spear

horrors (HOR-urz)—things that cause fear or shock

power (POU-ur)—great strength, energy, or the ability to do something

protect (pruh-TEKT)—to guard or shield something from harm

Rod of Iron (ROD UHV EYE-urn)—a powerful tool that can control the future of the world

Shadow Masters (SHAD-oh MASS-turz)—evil beings that control the darkness in the future; the Shadow Masters want to cover the earth in complete darkness.

shadows (SHAD-ohz)—shade or darkness caused by something blocking the light

DISCUSSION QUESTIONS

1. Using both the pictures and words, what do you know about the Shadow Masters? Are they good or evil? What do they look like? What do they want?

2. The Dark Man doesn't know the girl, but he decides to trust her. Why do you think he trusted this stranger? Do you believe this decision was good or bad?

3. At the end of the story, the girl is gone. What do you think happened to her? Do you believe she has the Rod of Iron? Why or why not?

WRITING PROMPTS

1. The old man says that the Rod of Iron can control the future. What would you do with the Rod of Iron? Describe how you would use it and what your future would be like.

2. What do you think the Rod of Iron looks like? Describe the size, weight, color, and other features of the Rod of Iron — maybe even draw a picture.

3. The author gives only a little information about the mysterious girl. Using your imagination, write more about this character. What is the girl's name? Where did she come from? How does she know where to find the Rod of Iron?

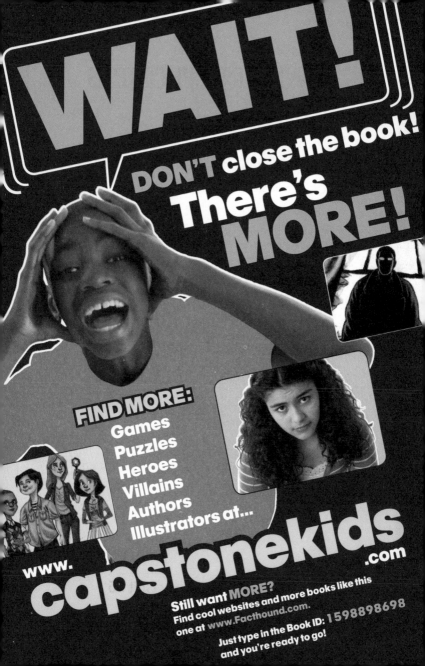

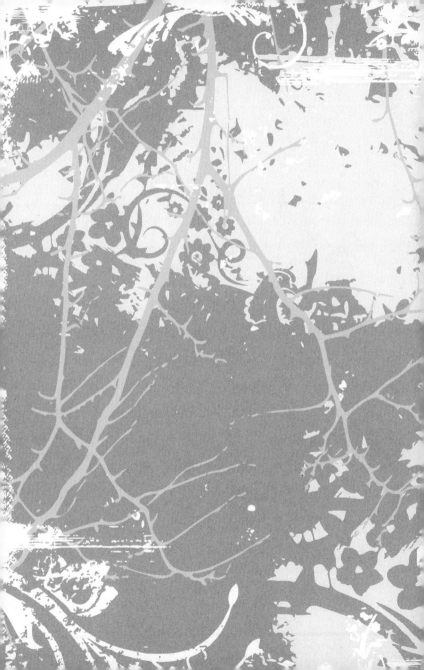

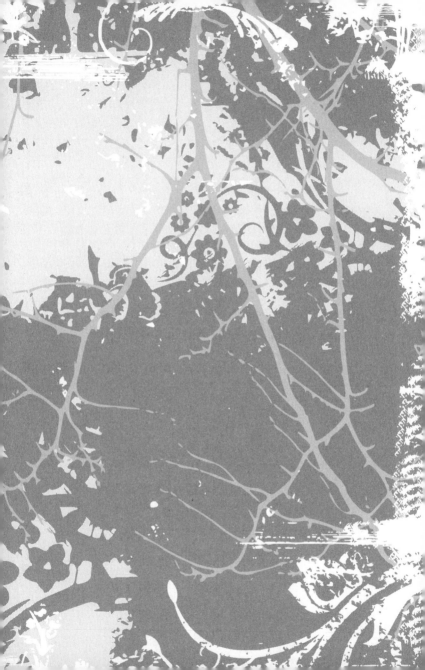